For Lauren and Lena

—M.R.

To providence hidden in tragic circumstances.
It points to yet another opportunity to fully realize this book.

—E.Y.

Kosho Hannya Wo Danzu.

An old pine tree can teach you the sacred truths.

— Zen Proverb

WABI SABI is a way of seeing the world that is at the heart of Japanese culture. It finds beauty and harmony in what is simple, imperfect, natural, modest, and mysterious. It can be a little dark, but it is also warm and comfortable. It may best be understood as a feeling, rather than as an idea.

Wabi Sabi

侘び寂び

MARK REIBSTEIN

ART BY ED YOUNG

LITTLE, BROWN AND COMPANY
Books for Young Readers
New York Boston

Wabi Sabi was a cat who lived in Kyoto, Japan. One day, visitors from another country asked Wabi Sabi's master what her name meant. It had never occurred to her before that wabi sabi was anything more than her name. Wabi Sabi watched as her master drew breath through her teeth, shook her head, and said: "That's hard to explain."

張抜きの猫も知るなり今朝の秋

The cat's tail twitching,
she watches her master, still
waiting in silence.

Curious now, Wabi Sabi wondered if her friend Snowball could explain the meaning of her name to her. Snowball, who had been napping, stretched, yawned, and sighed, "That's hard to explain." She blinked. "It's a kind of beauty," she added after a minute, her eyes closing again. As though dreaming, she went on:

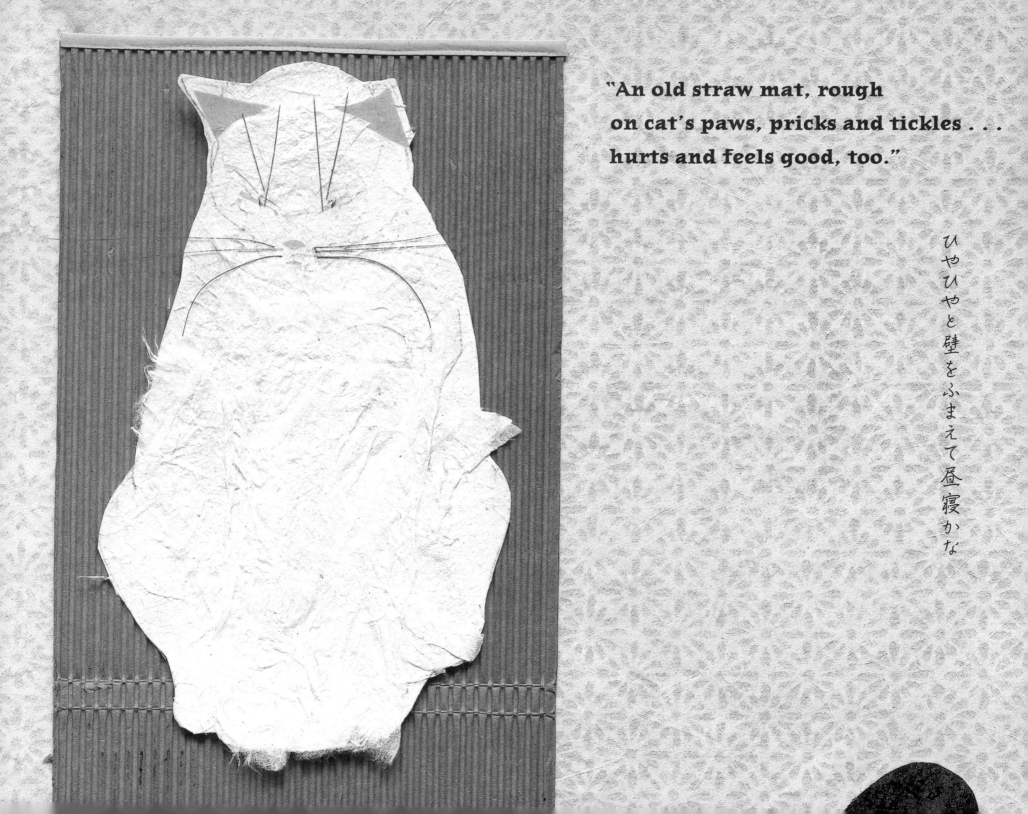

**"An old straw mat, rough
on cat's paws, pricks and tickles . . .
hurts and feels good, too."**

ひやひやと壁をふまえて昼寝かな

Then Snowball went back to sleep. Wabi Sabi wasn't sure she understood, but she didn't want to bother Snowball anymore. So she asked Rascal, the dog, if he knew about wabi sabi: Rascal was smart, but kind of mean. "That's too hard to explain to someone like you," he snapped. Then, almost to himself, he said:

"Poor Wabi Sabi!
As simple as a brown leaf.
So ordinary!"

物言えば唇寒し秋の風

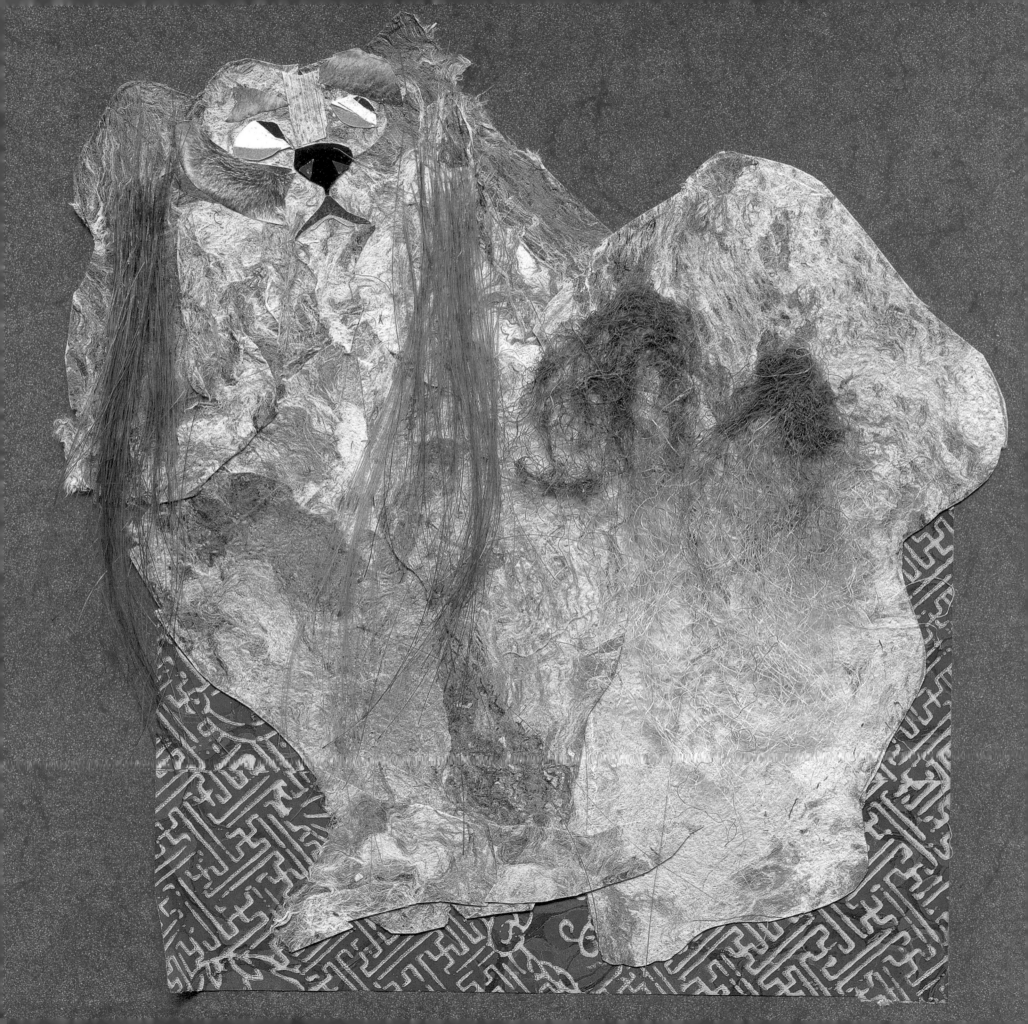

"Now I'm even more confused," sighed Wabi Sabi. "Am I beautiful or ordinary? Can anyone explain wabi sabi to me?" she cried.

A bird flying by thought the question was for her. "That's hard to explain," she said to Wabi Sabi. "But there is someone who can help you. His name is Kosho, and he lives on Mount Hiei, to the east.

**"A wise old monkey
living among the pine trees
knows wabi sabi."**

鳥啼いて赤き木の実をこぼしけり

この道を行く人なしに秋の暮

"Thank you!" said Wabi Sabi, and off she went to learn what her name meant.
To get to Mount Hiei, she had to cross through the city. Dazzled by big buildings,
shiny glass, and sleek cars, awed by the busy, sharply dressed people, she wondered
if these pretty things could be wabi sabi. She decided that if her name was true to
her, it must be softer, quieter, darker.

Even in cities,
before the shock of new light —
the colors of dusk.

A short time after Wabi Sabi entered the woods, she arrived at the foot of Mount Hiei. The woods were dark now, so, hoping to find Kosho in the morning, she curled up beneath an old pine tree and went to sleep. She awoke to the sounds of a stick stirring and tapping.

A warm bowl of tea
offered by a monkey, "Please!"
Steam rising gently.

松一ツ　影もつ月夜哉

Very glad to have the tea and company, she said, "Thank you.
My name is Wabi Sabi."

"That's wonderful!" the monkey replied.

Encouraged, she asked, "Do you know what that means?"

"Well, that's . . ." he began.

"I know, hard to explain," she said. But he went on:

**"The pale moon resting
on foggy water. Hear that
splash? A frog's jumped in."**

朝茶飲む僧静かなり菊の花

"That's wabi sabi?" she asked. "Is that all? I don't know if I can . . ."

"It's more," said the monkey. "Listen. Watch. Feel." He said no more, so she watched him make tea. He moved slowly but gracefully, as if he were dancing, and he handled his things as if they were gold, although they were wooden or clay. Wabi Sabi felt what was in her paws:

A warm heavy bowl
comfortable as an old friend —
not fine, smooth china.

She looked carefully at the woods surrounding them. There was so much life, as in the city, but here things were not clean, neat, or sharp-edged. There were no straight lines, yet there were many designs—on trees, in clouds and dirty ponds. She saw that everything was

**alive and dying
too, like the damp autumn leaves
curled beneath their feet.**

秋雨や水さびのたまる庭の池

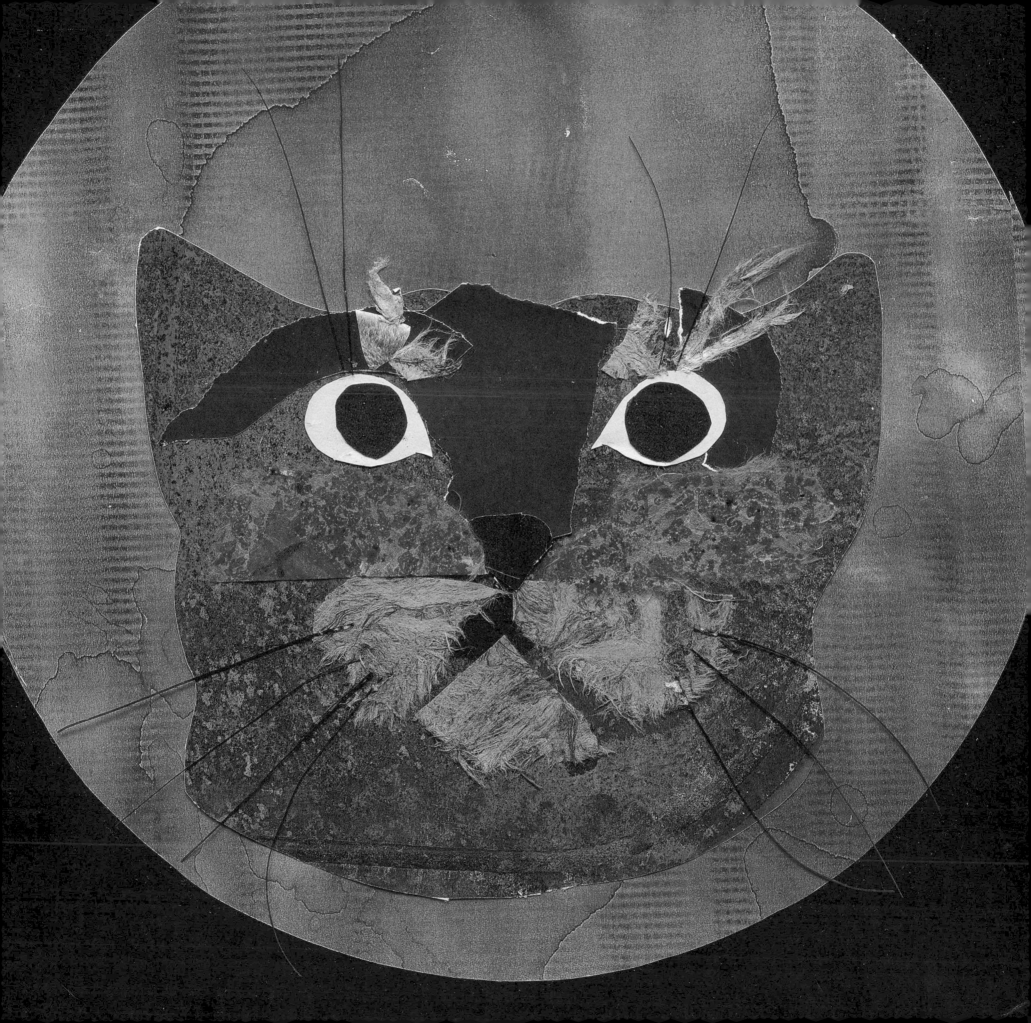

"Simple things are beautiful," she heard the monkey say as he poured more tea for her. Looking down at the tea in her bowl,

**seeing herself plain
and beautiful, she whispered,
"Now I understand."**

行く我にとゞまる汝に秋二つ

After some time, Wabi Sabi thanked her new friend and started back for home. Because she did not hurry, she found a place called Ginkakuji, the "Silver Temple.",

There was nothing silver there, but she found the place to be very beautiful — in a wabi sabi kind of way. Although the buildings and gardens were shaped by humans, they were neither fancy nor grand. Moved by the natural simplicity of the place, Wabi Sabi composed three short poems about what she saw:

赤蜻蛉地蔵の顔の夕日かな

Yellow bamboo stalks
bow by teahouse doors so low
emperors must kneel.

Dark buildings, floating,
sit on white sand seas. A stream
sweeps small stones, chanting.

The monk returns leaves
to just-raked sand. This humble
cat might understand.

Tired but glad, Wabi Sabi returned at last to her house. She curled up on the straw mat in the kitchen, enjoying the warmth there. She could smell the wind in her fur and feel her long journey's steps deep in her bones.

**The sun's last rays stretch
a silver brushstroke shivers
on warm clouded glass.**

"Now I think I know what to call this feeling," she said to herself. "It's . . . "

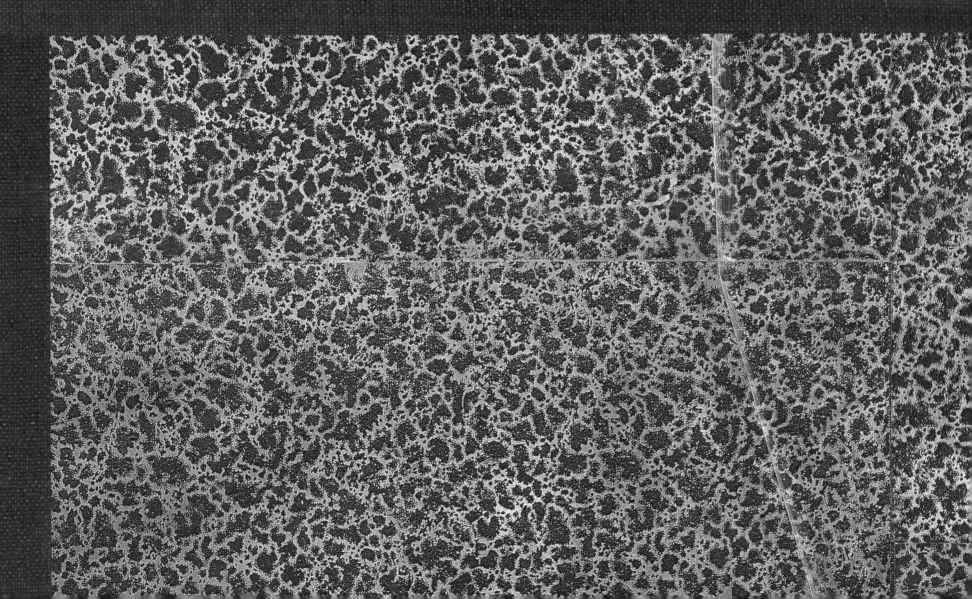

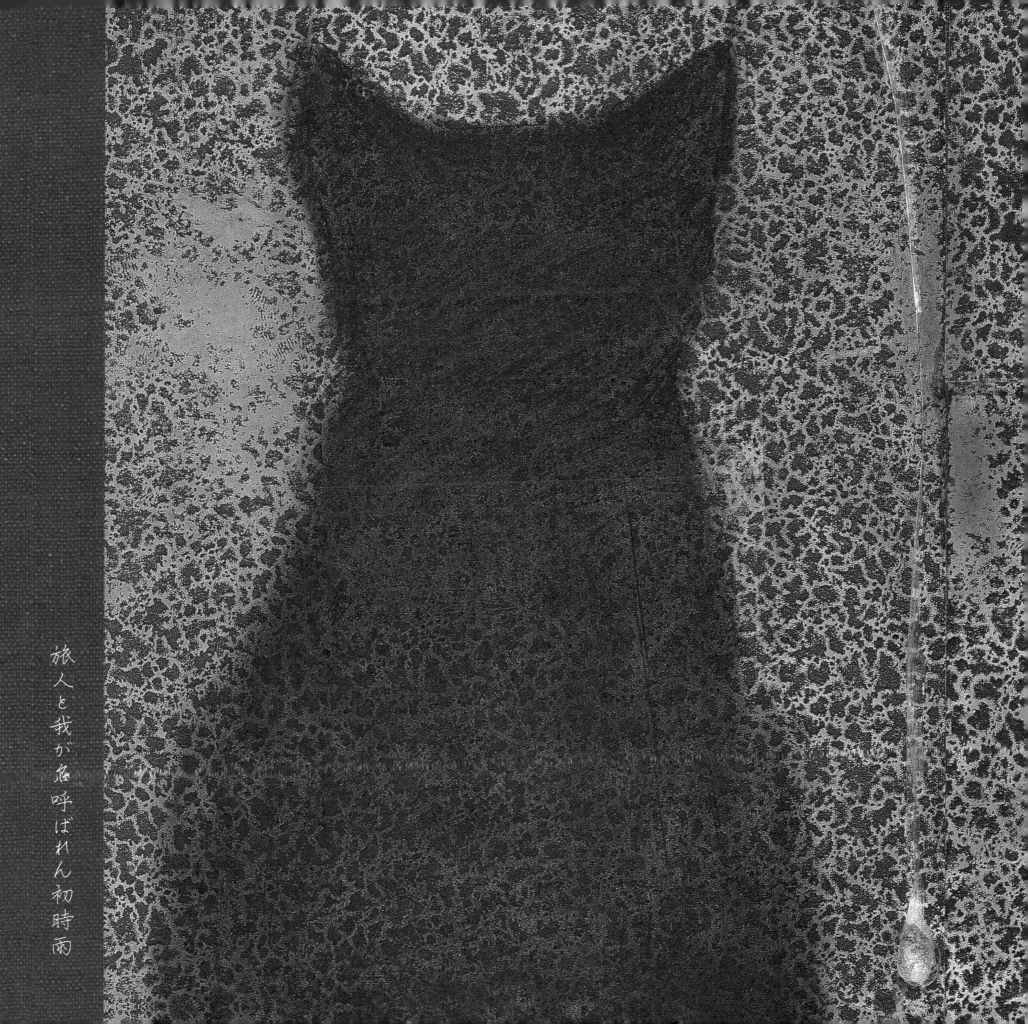

旅人と我が名呼ばれん初時雨

金屏の松の古さよ冬籠り

"Wabi Sabi!" cried her master, seeing her. "Where have you been?"
"That's hard to explain," she purred, feeling simply and beautifully at home.

THE HISTORY OF WABI SABI

Wabi sabi's origins are in ancient Chinese ways of understanding and living, known as Taoism and Zen Buddhism, but wabi sabi began to shape Japanese culture when the Zen priest Murata Shuko of Nara (1423–1502) changed the tea ceremony. He discarded the fancy gold, jade, and porcelain of the popular Chinese tea service, and introduced simple, rough, wooden and clay instruments. About a hundred years later, the famous tea master Sen no Rikyu of Kyoto (1522–1591) brought wabi sabi into the homes of the powerful. He constructed a teahouse with a door so low that even the emperor would have to bow in order to enter, reminding everyone of the importance of humility before tradition, mystery, and spirit.

HAIKU AND HAIBUN

A haiku is a short, traditional Japanese poem, which can be approximated in English by writing a first line of five syllables, a second of seven, and a third of five again. Meaning is usually expressed through details of the senses and of nature, with a seasonal reference and a transition of some kind that might make you think more deeply about those details. Matsuo Basho (1644–1694) may be the greatest haiku writer. Many of his haiku were written in the haibun form, where short prose passages set up each haiku. He recorded some of his epic journeys in this way. Perhaps the most famous haiku ever written is the one about the frog jumping in the water translated below by Masaoka Shiki (1867–1902), who is sometimes referred to as the last of the four great haiku masters. He helped make Basho and the haiku form popular in more modern times.

古池や蛙飛び込む水の音

Furuikeya kawazu tobikomu mizu no oto.
(the old mere!/a frog jumping in,/the sound of water.)

There are Japanese haiku that appear decoratively throughout this book. They were written by Basho (indicated with Ⓑ) and Shiki (indicated with Ⓢ) and are translated below. They were chosen and translated into English by Nanae Tamura. Ms. Tamura, a haiku scholar, translator, and author, judges a national haiku competition in Japan and is an International Exchange Associate at the International Center, Ehime University.

Ⓑ **1.** 張抜きの猫も知るなり今朝の秋
Harinuki no neko mo shirunari kesano-aki

Ⓑ **2.** ひやひやと壁をふまえて昼寝かな
Hiyahiyato kabe o fumaete hirune kana

Ⓑ **3.** 物言えば唇寒し秋の風
Mono ieba kuchibiru samushi aki no kaze

Ⓢ **4.** 鳥啼いて赤き木の実をこぼしけり
Tori naite akaki kinomi o koboshikeri

Ⓑ **5.** この道を行く人なしに秋の暮
Konomichi o yuku hito nashini aki no kure

Ⓢ **6.** 松一ツ　影もつ月夜哉
Matsu hitotsu hitotsu kage motsu tsukiyo kana

Ⓑ **7.** 名月や池をめぐりて夜もすがら
Meigetsu ya ike o megurite yo mo sugara

Ⓑ **8.** 朝茶飲む僧静かなり菊の花
Asa-cha nomu sō shizukanari kiku no hana

Ⓢ **9.** 秋雨や水さびのたまる庭の池
Akisame ya misabi no tamaru niwa no ike

Ⓢ **10.** 行く我にとゞまる汝に秋二つ
Yuku ware ni todomaru nare ni aki futatsu

Ⓢ **11.** 赤蜻蛉地蔵の顔の夕日かな
Akatombo jizo no kao no yūhi kana

Ⓑ **12.** 庭掃いて出ばや寺に散る柳
Niwa haite idebaya tera ni chiru yanagi

Ⓑ **13.** 旅人と我が名呼ばれん初時雨
Tabibito to wagana yobaren hatsu-shigure

Ⓑ **14.** 金屏の松の古さよ冬籠り
Kimbyo no matsu no furusayo fuyugomori

1. even a papier-mâché cat
   knows it:
   the beginning of autumn

2. how comfortable
   touching the cool wall—
   a daytime nap

3. when speaking
   a chill on the lips:
   autumn wind

4. a bird chirps
   shaking
   red berries

5. along this road
   no one else goes. . . .
   autumn evening

6. each pine tree
   has its own shadow:
   the moonlit night

7. the full moon—
   going around the pond
   all night long

8. having morning tea
   a priest in deep silence:
   chrysanthemums

9. autumn rain . . .
   water-rust collects
   on the garden pond

10. for me leaving
    for you staying
    two autumns

11. a red dragonfly—
    the stone-buddha's face
    clothed in the evening glow

12. on leaving the temple
    where I swept:
    falling willow leaves

13. a traveler
    I may be called:
    the first winter drizzle

14. how venerable, the pine
    on the gilded folding screen:
    winter seclusion

Thanks to Roni Schotter, Izumi Kamata,
Nanae Tamura, Miho Minami, Roger Cook,
Yuki Tsujuika, Kiyo Thittipanyakul,
Alvina Ling, and the Hacklers!
—M.R.

A collection of time-worn human-made as
well as natural materials were used for my
collages, thanks to the generosity of Harry
Bolick, Antonia Young, and Cathleen Chou.
—E.Y.

Little, Brown and Company

Hachette Book Group USA
237 Park Avenue, New York, NY 10017
Visit our Web site at www.lb-kids.com

First Edition: October 2008

Library of Congress Cataloging-in-Publication Data

Reibstein, Mark.
  Wabi Sabi / by Mark Reibstein ; [illustrations] by Ed Young — 1st
ed.
    p. cm.
  Summary: Wabi Sabi, a cat living in the city of Kyoto, learns about
the Japanese concept of beauty through simplicity as she asks various
animals she meets about the meaning of her name.
  ISBN 978-0-316-11825-5
  [1. Cats—Fiction. 2. Aesthetics, Japanese—Fiction. 3.
Animals—Fiction. 4. Japan—Fiction.] I. Young, Ed, ill. II. Title.
  PZ7.R262Wa 2008
  [E]—dc22
                        2007050895

10 9 8 7 6 5 4 3

TWP

Printed in Singapore

The text was set in Journal Text,
and the display type was hand-cut.